Michelle, Elijah, and Sonny, with love
G.P.-P.

This edition published by Parragon in 2013
Parragon
Chartist House
15-17 Trim Street
Bath BA1 1HA, UK
www.parragon.com

Published by arrangement with Gullane Children's Books
185 Fleet Street, London, EC4A 2HS

Text © Giles Paley-Phillips 2013
Illustrations © Liz Pichon 2013

ISBN 978-1-4723-1116-0

Printed in China

THINGS YOU NEVER KNEW About DINOSAURS

Giles
Paley-Phillips

illustrated by
Liz Pichon

PaRragon

Bath · New York · Singapore · Hong Kong · Cologne · Delhi
Melbourne · Amsterdam · Johannesburg · Shenzhen

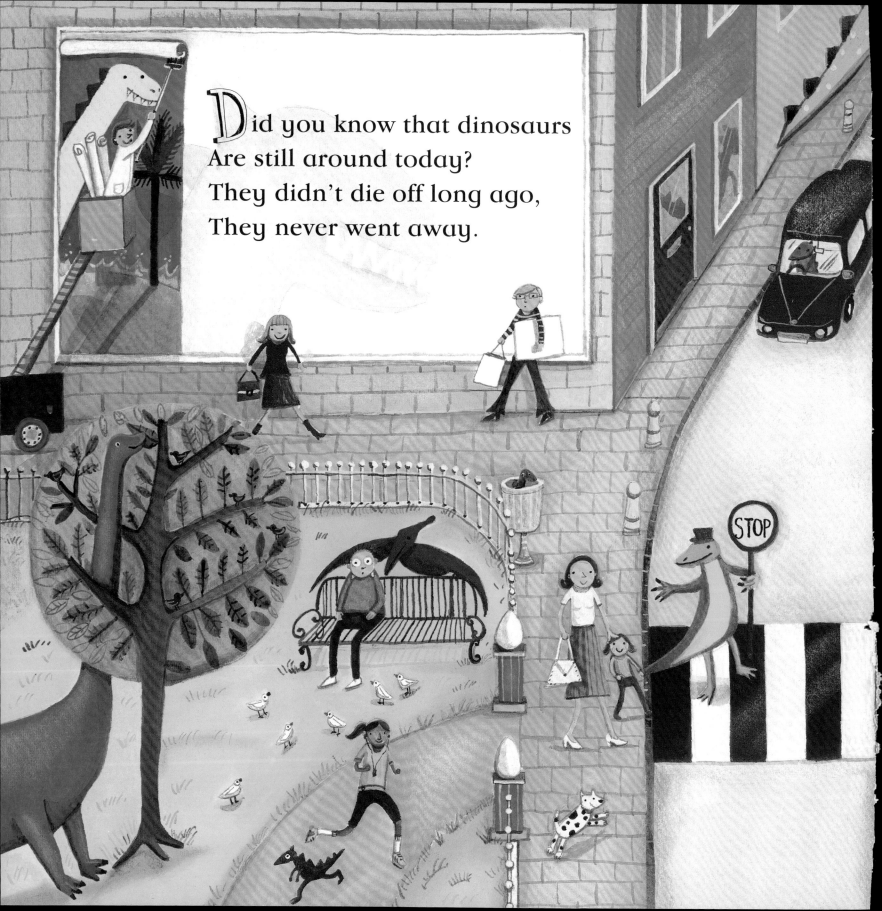

Did you know that dinosaurs
Are still around today?
They didn't die off long ago,
They never went away.

On every street in every town,
Maybe next door to you,
Dinosaurs are doing things
You won't BELIEVE are true...

Dinosaurs play tennis.

They ride around on bikes.

They
like
to
bounce
on

and go for hilltop hikes.

Dinosaurs love to play guitar,

To stomp their feet and sing.

They love to waltz and
cha cha cha
And do the Highland fling.

There are some things they DON'T like much,
Things they really HATE!
Dinosaurs don't like doing math ...

You'll never see them brush their teeth
Or clean their dirty plates.
And when they should be fast asleep,
They're whizzing around on skates!

DINOSAUR
of the
Caribbean

Some dinosaurs go up in space
To see the Moon and Mars.

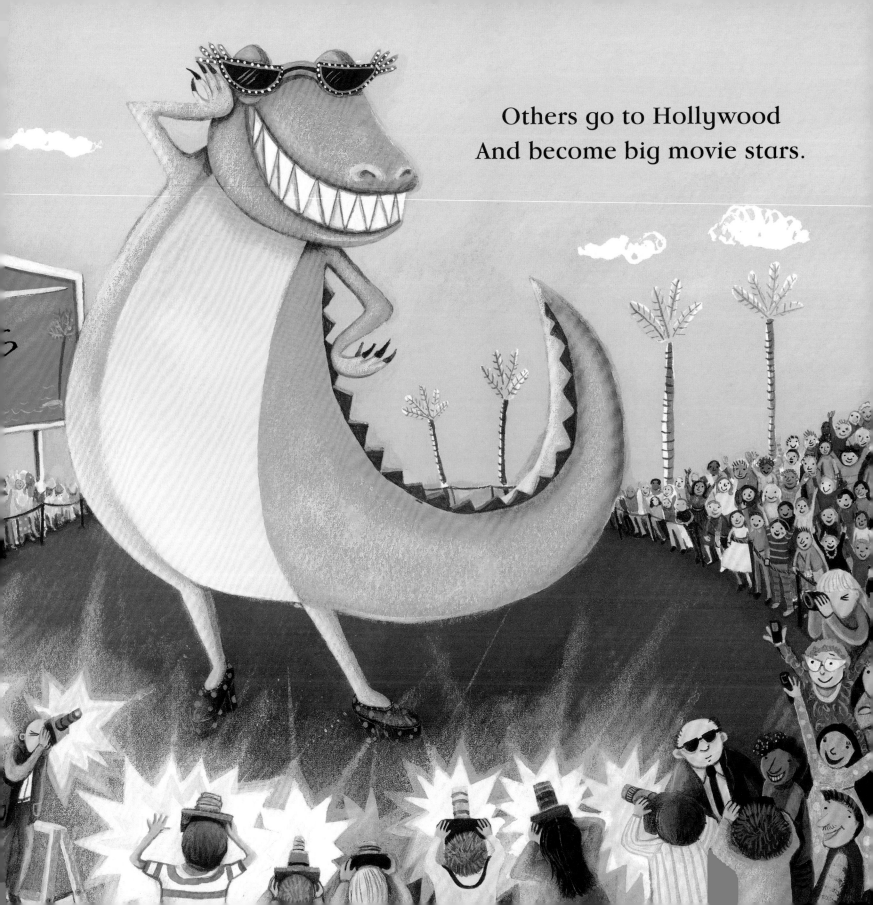

Others go to Hollywood
And become big movie stars.

Dinosaurs sail the seven seas,

They trek from pole to pole...

And in the World Cup final
One scored the **winning goal.**

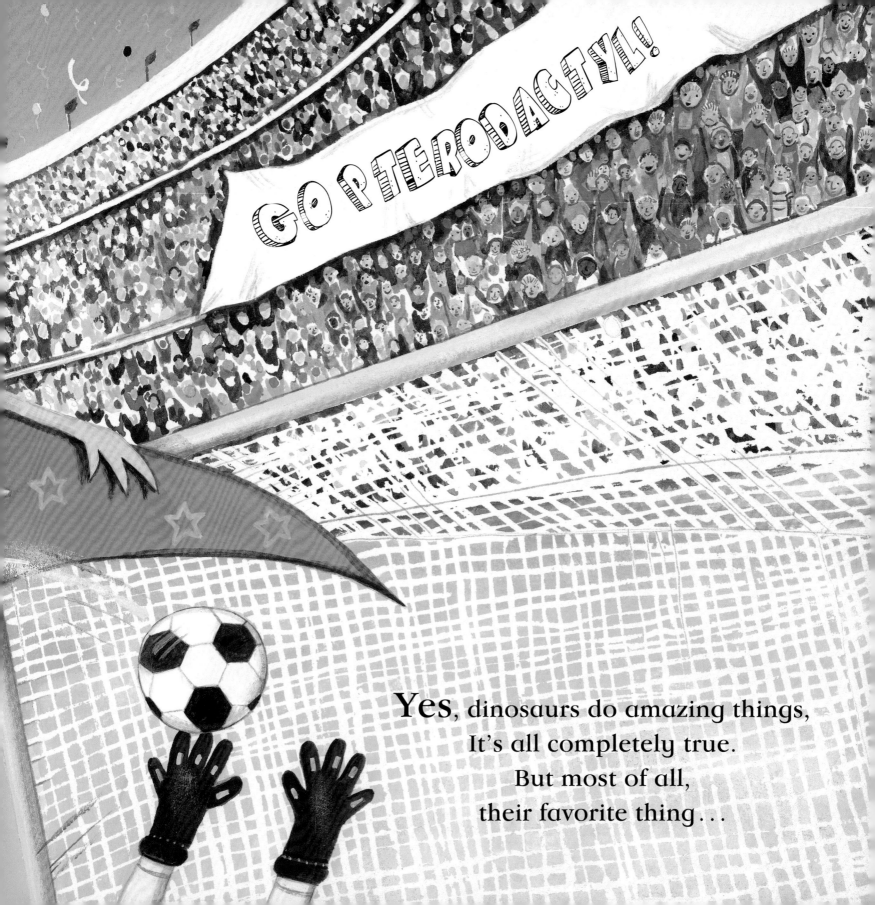

GO PTERODACTYL!

Yes, dinosaurs do amazing things,
It's all completely true.
But most of all,
their favorite thing...